AMAZING
AIRPLANES

For Jan and Billy—T. M.
For Henry and Horace—A. P.

The Publisher thanks the British Airways Community Learning Center at
Heathrow Airport in London, England, for their kind assistance in the development of this book.

KINGFISHER
LONDON & NEW YORK

Distributed in the U.S. and Canada by Macmillan,
120 Broadway, New York, NY 10271

Kingfisher books are available for special promotions and premiums.
For details contact: Special Markets Department, Macmillan,
120 Broadway, New York, NY 10271

For more information, please visit www.kingfisherbooks.com

library of congress cataloging-in-publication data
Mitton, Tony.
Amazing Machines/Tony Mitton and Ant Parker.
p. cm.—(Amazing machines)
1. Airplanes—Juvenile literature.
2. Air travel—Juvenile literature.
I. Parker, Ant. II. Title. III. Series.
TL547.M638 2005
387.7'3—dc22 2005027408

ISBN: 978-0-7534-5403-9

Printed in China
10

AMAZING AIRPLANES

Tony Mitton and
Ant Parker

KINGFISHER
LONDON & NEW YORK

Whoosh

An airplane is amazing,
for it travels through the sky,

above the clouds for miles and miles,
so very fast and high!

An airport is the place you go
to take a trip by air.

You check in at the terminal to show
you've paid your fare.

The ground crew weighs your baggage
and loads it in the hold.

And then you take the walkway to the plane
when you are told.

The flight deck's where the captain
and copilot do their jobs.
They both know how to fly the plane
with all its dials and knobs.

They radio Control Tower to check
the runway's clear.
They can't take off unless it is,
with other planes so near.

By intercom the captain on the flight deck
says hello.

You have to put your seat belt on
before the plane can go!

A plane is big and heavy,
yet it climbs up really high.

It zooms along the runway
and soars into the sky.

whoosh

Its wings hold big jet engines,
which are loud and very strong.
They suck in air and blow it through
to whoosh the plane along.

When the plane moves fast enough,
the air around's so swift
it pushes up beneath the wings
and makes the whole plane lift.

Soon the plane is in the air,
so now you're on your flight.
The cabin crew look after you
and make sure you're all right.

They bring you drinks and magazines
and trays of food to eat.
And sometimes there's a movie
you can watch while in your seat.

When the journey's over,
the captain lands the plane.
Control Tower has to say it's safe
for coming down again.

You sit with seat belt fastened,
there's a bumpy, rumbling sound—
the wheels are making contact,
and the plane is on the ground!

At last the doors are opening.
Then out you come with smiles.

So give a cheer. Hooray—you're here!
You've flown for miles and miles.

Airplane parts

control tower
from here the air traffic controllers direct the planes and tell pilots when to take off and land safely

flight deck
sometimes called the **cockpit**, this is where the pilot and copilot sit

wheel
the wheels fold away while the plane is in the air

hold
this is the space where heavy luggage is stored

jet engine
jet engines blow out air and gas to push the plane forward—the gas is made by burning fuel

wing
the wings are hollow to make them as light as possible and a smooth shape so they move through the air easily

terminal
this is the building at the airport where passengers go to catch a plane

Collect all the **AMAZING MACHINES** books by Tony Mitton and Ant Parker!

HC ISBN 978-0-7534-7457-0
TP ISBN 978-0-7534-7458-7
BB ISBN 978-0-7534-7494-5

HC ISBN 978-0-7534-5403-9
TP ISBN 978-0-7534-5915-7
BB ISBN 978-0-7534-7370-2

TP ISBN 978-0-7534-5916-4
BB ISBN 978-0-7534-7416-7

HC ISBN 978-0-7534-5802-0
TP ISBN 978-0-7534-7207-1
BB ISBN 978-0-7534-7395-5

TP ISBN 978-0-7534-5304-9
BB ISBN 978-0-7534-7394-8

TP ISBN 978-0-7534-5307-0
BB ISBN 978-0-7534-7373-3

HC ISBN 978-0-7534-7290-3
TP ISBN 978-0-7534-7291-0
BB ISBN 978-0-7534-7418-1

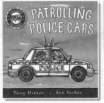

HC ISBN 978-0-7534-7292-7
TP ISBN 978-0-7534-7293-4
BB ISBN 978-0-7534-7419-8

HC ISBN 978-0-7534-7455-6
TP ISBN 978-0-7534-7456-3
BB ISBN 978-0-7534-7495-2

TP ISBN 978-0-7534-5305-6
BB ISBN 978-0-7534-7371-9

TP ISBN 978-0-7534-7208-8
BB ISBN 978-0-7534-7417-4

TP ISBN 978-0-7534-5306-3
BB ISBN 978-0-7534-7372-6

TP ISBN 978-0-7534-5917-1
BB ISBN 978-0-7534-7397-9

TP ISBN 978-0-7534-5918-8
BB ISBN 978-0-7534-7396-2

Younger children will love these **AMAZING MACHINES** tabbed board books:

ISBN 978-0-7534-7440-2

ISBN 978-0-7534-7439-6

Listen out for the sound book—with 10 airplane sounds!

ISBN 978-0-7534-7328-3

Get busy with the **AMAZING MACHINES** activity and sticker books:

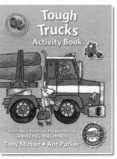

ISBN 978-0-7534-7255-2

ISBN 978-0-7534-7256-9

ISBN 978-0-7534-7257-6

ISBN 978-0-7534-7254-5